Lucky Clucky

Tony Blundell

PUFFIN BOOKS

Penguin Putnam Inc., 375 Hudson Street, New York, New York 10014, USA
Penguin Books Australia Ltd, 250 Camberwell Road, Camberwell, Victoria 3124, Australia
Penguin Books Canada Ltd, 10 Alcorn Avenue, Toronto, Ontario, Canada M4V 3B2
Penguin Books India (P) Ltd, 11 Community Centre, Panchsheel Park, New Delhi – 110 017, India
Penguin Books (NZ) Ltd, Cnr Rosedale and Airborne Roads, Albany, Auckland, New Zealand
Penguin Books (South Africa) (Pty) Ltd, 24 Sturdee Avenue, Rosebank 2196, South Africa

Penguin Books Ltd, Registered Offices: 80 Strand, London WC2R 0RL

www.penguin.com

First published by Viking 1999
Published in Puffin Books 2000
3 5 7 9 10 8 6 4

Copyright © Tony Blundell, 1999
All rights reserved

The moral right of the author/illustrator has been asserted

Made and printed in Italy by Printer Trento Srl

A CIP catalogue record for this book is available from the British Library
British Library Cataloguing in Publication Data

0–140–56461–6

Clucky, the little red hen, was feeling gloomy. It would be her birthday soon, but not one of the lazy creatures in the farmyard ever remembered.

"No cake, no funny hats and no party games," she clucked. "Not even a card! I suppose I'll just have to make my own birthday treat," she said.

And so she set to work.

"Who will help me sow some corn?"
asked Clucky, walking into the barn
with her apron full of seeds.

"Not I," purred the cat, "my fur needs a clean."
"Not I," quacked the duck, "I have feathers to preen."
"Not I," bleated the goat, "I am watching a snail."
"Not I," grunted the pig, "I've a curl in my tail."
"Not I," honked the goose, "I'm having a rest."
"Not I," baaed the sheep, "I am knitting a vest."
"Not us," they all said, "we have much too much to do."

And the Big Bad Wolf said ...

"Hi, Woolly – GUESS WHO!"

So the little red hen had to sow the corn all on her own, because somebody had to do it.

Soon the sun came out and the corn began to grow.

"Who will help me water the corn?" asked Clucky, a watering can under each wing.

"Not I," purred the cat, "I am washing my paws."
"Not I," quacked the duck, "I am painting my claws."
"Not I," bleated the goat, "I have my horns to scratch."
"Not I," grunted the pig, "I have forty winks to catch."
"Not I," honked the goose, "I'm admiring the view."
"Not us," they all said, "we have much too much to do."

And the Big Bad Wolf said ...

"Hi, Goosey – GUESS WHO!"

So the little red hen had to water the corn all on her own, because somebody had to do it.

Soon the corn grew high and dry enough to be cut.

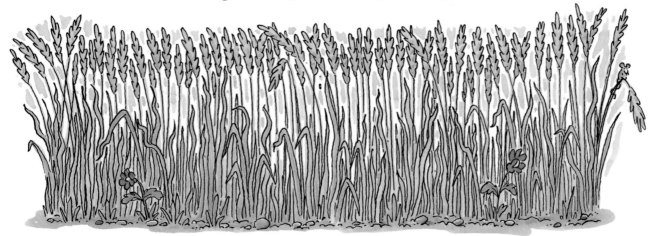

"Who will help me cut the corn?" asked Clucky, sharpening her scythe on a stone.

"Not I," purred the cat, "I've a twitch in my tail."
"Not I," quacked the duck, "there's a leak in my pail."
"Not I," bleated the goat, "I've my beard to sort out."
"Not I," grunted the pig, "I've a sneeze in my snout."
"Not us," they all said, "we have much too much to do."

And the Big Bad Wolf said ...

"Hi, Piggy – GUESS WHO!"

So the little red hen had to cut the corn all by herself, because somebody had to do it.

Soon all the corn was cut and raked into a pile.

"Who will help me grind the corn?" asked Clucky, puffing a bit after all her hard work.

"Not I," purred the cat, "I am watching the mice."
"Not I," quacked the duck, "my feet are like ice."
"Not I," bleated the goat, "I've a touch of the flu."
"Not us," they all said, "we have much too much to do."

And the Big Bad Wolf said ...

"Hi, Billy – GUESS WHO!"

So the little red hen had to grind the corn all on her own, because somebody had to do it.

Soon the corn was ground into a fine, fluffy flour.

"Who will help me make the dough?"
asked Clucky, brushing the flour
from her feathers.

"Not I," purred the cat, "it's time for a sleep."
"Not I," quacked the duck, "I'm looking for the sheep."
"Not us," they both said, "we have much too much to do."

And the Big Bad Wolf said ...

"Hi, Ducky – GUESS WHO!"

So the little red hen had to make the dough all on her own, because somebody had to do it.

Soon the dough was made and kneaded and pressed into a tin.

"Who will help me bake the bread?" asked Clucky, hopefully.

"Not I," purred the cat, "if it's all the same to you.
"Not I," the cat said, "I have much too much to do."

And the Big Bad Wolf said ...

"Hi, Kitty – GUESS WHO!"

So the little red hen had to bake the bread all on her own, because somebody had to do it.

Soon the bread was baked. Clucky stuck a candle in the top and set off for the barn.

There she found the Big Bad Wolf leaning against
the door and looking at her in a hungry sort of way.
"Who will help me eat the bread?" asked Clucky,
looking a little nervous.

"Not I," said the Big Bad Wolf, "I've much too much to do.
"Not I," said the Big Bad Wolf, "but I will eat ...

"... your birthday tea with you!"

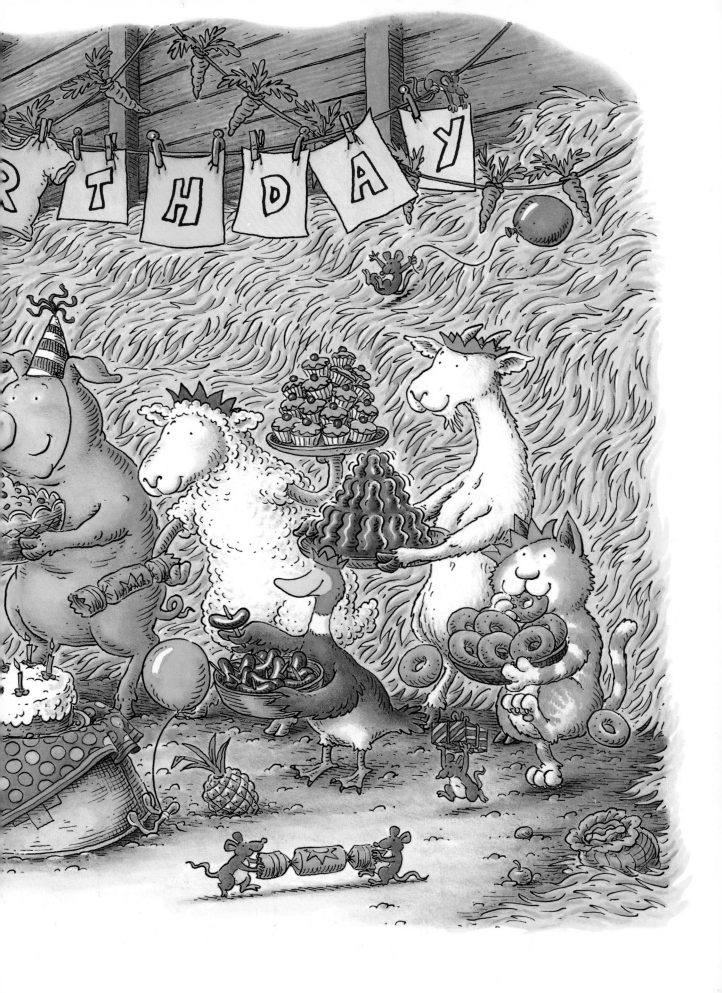

Happy Birthday,
Lucky Clucky!